The Berenstain Bears
and the
SITTER

Mom and Dad are going out,
Gramps and Gran are, too.
Who will stay home
with the cubs?
Just anyone won't do...

A FIRST TIME BOOK®

The Berenstain Bears and the SITTER

Stan & Jan Berenstain

Random House 🏠 New York

Library of Congress Cataloging in Publication Data: Berenstain, Stan [date]. The Berenstain Bears and the sitter. (Berenstain Bears first time books / Stan Berenstain) SUMMARY: Brother and Sister Bear are not happy with the idea of Mrs. Grizzle for a baby-sitter, but they find her drawstring bag very intriguing. [1. Baby-sitters—Fiction. 2. Bears—Fiction] I. Berenstain, Jan [date]. II. Title. PZ7.B4483Bej [E] AACR2 81-50046 ISBN: 0-394-84837-3 (trade); 0-394-94837-8 (lib. bdg.) Manufactured in the United States of America

26 27 28 29 30

"What's this?" said Papa Bear, as he took the day's mail from the Bear Family's mailbox.

It was a notice telling about an important meeting that night at the Bear Country Town Hall.

Mama Bear called up Grizzly Gran. Brother and Sister Bear sometimes stayed with Gramps and Gran when Mama and Papa Bear had to be away.

But Gramps and Gran were planning to go to the meeting, too. So Brother and Sister couldn't stay with them.

Or with Aunt Maude . . .

or Cousin Wilbur.
They were going to the
meeting, too.

"Why can't we go with you?" asked Sister, beginning to get a little upset.

"Yeah!" added Brother Bear.

"Because," said Papa, "this meeting is for grown-ups. And, besides, it won't be over until late—way past your bedtime."

"Well, where are we going to stay?" the cubs wanted to know.

"You're going to stay right here,"
said Mama, as she put down the phone.

"Alone?" asked Sister.

"Of course not," said Mama.
"I've arranged for a sitter."

"A sitter?!" said Brother.

"Who is it going to be?"
Sister asked.

"Mrs. Grizzle, who lives
in the hollow stump at the
end of the road," said Mama,
feeling much better about
the whole thing.

"Mrs. Grizzle!" said the
cubs, not feeling better
at all. . . .

Once, when Sister was playing with her friends, their ball went into Mrs. Grizzle's flower garden. Mrs. Grizzle wasn't too happy about it.

And another time, when Brother was flying his kite, it swooped and bumped Mrs. Grizzle on the hat.

She wasn't too tickled about that, either.

Later that evening, after the supper things had been cleaned up, Mama and Papa got ready to go to the town meeting.

"But who's going to scrub our backs, read us a story, and tuck us in?" asked Sister, still a little nervous about the idea of a sitter.

"I understand that Mrs. Grizzle has raised seven cubs of her own," said Mama, putting on her hat. "And I'm sure she's a perfectly good back scrubber, story reader, and tucker-inner."

"She's not going to scrub *my* back!" Brother Bear said under his breath.

Mrs. Grizzle came walking up the path to the Bears' tree house right on time.

There was no question about it. It was the same Mrs. Grizzle who got bopped with the kite and didn't like cubs tromping her flowers.

She was very large—almost as big as Papa— and she carried a drawstring bag.

"Evenin', all!" said Mrs. Grizzle in a loud, jolly voice. "Well, time's a-wastin', you two!" she said to Mama and Papa. "You better skedaddle off to your meetin'!"

Mrs. Grizzle had a strong way of saying things, and folks usually did what she said.

Mama and Papa kissed the cubs good night—and skedaddled.

"Whew!" said Mrs. Grizzle, as she sat down in Papa's big chair. "It sure is good to get a load off your feet!" She took off her hat and looked into her drawstring bag.

There's something about somebody looking into a bag that makes cubs very curious.

"Mrs. Grizzle?" said Sister.

"Yes?"

"What's in the bag?"

"Nothin' much. Just some things I take along when I go sittin'—a piece of string, a pack of cards . . . "

Meanwhile, over at the Town Hall, the bears were getting ready for their important meeting.

They were getting ready for speeches, voting, and arguments about some new laws.

But Mama's mind was not on the meeting. Neither was Papa's. Mama and Papa Bear were thinking about what was going on back home.

"Sister looked a little worried when we left," fretted Mama.

"So did Brother," agreed Papa.

They decided to call home and see how things were going.

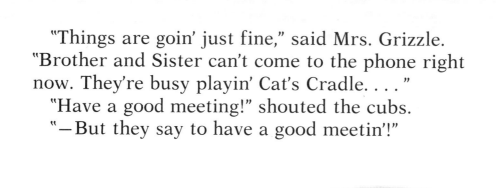

"Things are goin' just fine," said Mrs. Grizzle.
"Brother and Sister can't come to the phone right
now. They're busy playin' Cat's Cradle. . . . "
   "Have a good meeting!" shouted the cubs.
   "—But they say to have a good meetin'!"

After Cat's Cradle, they played Go Fish with the cards that came out of Mrs. Grizzle's drawstring bag.

Then they played Tiddly-winks with a special set of winks that Mrs. Grizzle had made out of polished stones and a snail-shell cup.

After a while, the cubs got the yawns, and Mrs. Grizzle began getting them ready for bed.

And she did, indeed, turn out to be a very good back scrubber (Brother changed his mind about not having his back scrubbed). . . .

And she was
a fine story reader . . .

and a really super
tucker-inner.

The cubs had a number of different sitters
from time to time, but Mrs. Grizzle was their
favorite—and they were always glad to see her.